MW00471569

Spanking the Maid

SPANKING THE MAID

A Novel by
ROBERT COOVER

Grove Press   New York

Published simultaneously in Canada
Printed in the United States of America

Library of Congress Cataloging-in-Publication Data

ISBN 0-7394-2079-8

Grove Press
841 Broadway
New York, NY 10003

Spanking the Maid

She enters, deliberately, gravely, without affectation, circumspect in her motions (as she's been taught), not stamping too loud, nor dragging her legs after her, but advancing sedately, discreetly, glancing briefly at the empty rumpled bed, the cast-off nightclothes. She hesitates. No. Again. She enters. Deliberately and gravely, without affectation, not stamping too loud, nor dragging her legs after her, not marching as if leading a dance, nor keeping time with her head and hands, nor staring or turning her head either one way or the other, but advancing sedately and discreetly through the door, across the polished floor, past the empty rumpled bed and cast-off nightclothes (not glancing, that's better), to the tall curtains along the far wall. As she's been taught. Now, with a humble yet authoritative gesture, she draws the curtains open: Ah! the morning sunlight comes flooding in over the gleaming tiles as though (she thinks) flung from a bucket. She opens wide the glass doors behind the curtains (there is such a song of birds all about!) and gazes for a moment into the garden, quite prepared to let the sweet breath of morning blow in and excite her to the most generous and efficient accomplishments, but her mind is still locked on that image, at first pleasing, now troubling, of the light as it spilled into the room: as from a bucket . . . . She sighs. She enters. With a bucket. She sets the bucket down, deliberately, gravely, and walks (circumspectly) across the room, over the polished tiles, past the empty rumpled bed (she doesn't glance at it), to draw open the tall curtains at the far wall. Buckets of light come flooding in (she is not thinking about this now) and the room, as she opens wide the glass doors, is sweetened by the fresh morning air blowing in from the garden. The sun is fully risen and the pink clouds of dawn are all gone out of the sky (the time lost: this is what she is thinking about), but the dew is still on every plant in the garden, and everything looks clean and bright. As will his room when she is done with it.

He awakes from a dream (something about utility, or futility, and a teacher he once had who, when he whipped his students, called it his "civil service"), still wrapped in darkness and hugged close to the sweet breast of the night, but with the new day already hard upon him, just beyond the curtains (he knows, even without looking), waiting for him out there like a brother: to love him or to kill him. He pushes the bed-covers back and sits up groggily to meet its challenge (or promise), pushes his feet into slippers, rubs his face, stretches, wonders what new blunders the maid (where is she?) will commit today. Well. I should at least give her a chance, he admonishes himself with a gaping yawn.

Oh, she knows her business well: to scrub and wax the floors, polish the furniture, make the master's bed soft and easy, lay up his nightclothes, wash, starch, and mend the bedlinens as necessary, air the blankets and clean the bathroom, making certain of ample supplies of fresh towels and washcloths, soap, toilet paper, razor blades and toothpaste—in short, to see that nothing be wanting which he desires or requires to be done, being always diligent in endeavoring to please him, silent when he is angry except to beg his pardon, and ever faithful, honest, submissive, and of good disposition.

The trivial round, the common task, she knows as she sets about her morning's duties, will furnish all she needs to ask, room to deny herself, a road (speaking loosely) to bring her daily nearer God. But on that road, on the floor of the bathroom, she finds a damp towel and some pajama bottoms, all puddled together like a cast-off mop-head. Mop-head? She turns and gazes in dismay at the empty bucket by the outer door. Why, she wants to know, tears springing to the corners of her eyes, can't it be easier than this? And so she enters, sets her bucket down with a firm deliberation, leans her mop gravely against the wall. Also a broom, brushes, some old rags, counting things off on her fingers as she deposits them. The curtains have been drawn open and the room is already (as though impatiently) awash with morning sunlight. She crosses the room, past the (no glances) empty rumpled bed, and opens wide the glass

doors leading out into the garden, letting
in the sweet breath of morning, which she
hardly notices. She has resolved this morning—as every morning—to be cheerful and
good-natured, such that if any accident
should happen to test that resolution, she
should not suffer it to put her out of temper with everything besides, but such reso-
lutions are more easily sworn than obeyed.
Things are already in such a state! Yet:
virtue is made for difficulties, she reminds
herself, and grows stronger and brighter
for such trials. *"Oh, teach me, my God and
King, in all things thee to see, and what I do
in any thing, to do it as for thee!"* she sings
out to the garden and to the room, feeling
her heart lift like a sponge in a bucket. *"A
servant with this clause makes drudgery divine: who sweeps a room, as for thy laws, makes
that and th'action fine!"* And yes, she can
still recover the lost time. She has everything now, the mop and bucket, broom,
rags and brushes, her apron pockets are

full of polishes, dustcloths and cleaning powders, the cupboards are well stocked with fresh linens, all she really needs now is to keep—but ah! is there, she wonders anxiously, spinning abruptly on her heels as she hears the master relieving himself noisily in the bathroom, any *water* in the bucket—?!

He awakes, squints at his watch in the darkness, grunts (she's late, but just as well, time for a shower), and with only a moment's hesitation, tosses the blankets back, tearing himself free: I'm so old, he thinks, and still every morning is a bloody new birth. Somehow it should be easier than this. He sits up painfully (that divine government!), rubs his face, pushes his feet into slippers, stands, stretches, then strides to the windows at the far wall and throws open the tall curtains, letting the sun in. The room seems almost to explode with the blast of light: he resists, then surrenders to, finally welcomes its amicable violence. He opens wide the glass doors that lead out into the garden and stands there in the sunshine, sucking in deeply the fresh morning air and trying to recall the dream he's just had. Something about a teacher who had once lectured him on humility. Severely. Only now, in the dream, he was himself the teacher and the student was a woman he knew, or thought he knew, and in his lecture "humility" kept getting mixed up somehow with "humor," such that, in effect, he was trying, in all severity, to teach her how to laugh. He's standing there in the sunlight in his slippers and pajama bottoms, remembering the curious strained expression on the woman's face as she tried—desperately, it seemed—to laugh, and wondering why this provoked (in the dream) such a fury in him, when the maid comes in. She gazes impassively a moment (yet humbly, circumspectly) at the gaping fly of his pajamas, then turns away, sets her bucket down against the wall. Her apron strings are loose, there's a hole in one of her black stockings, and she's forgotten her mop again. I'd be a happier man, he acknowledges to himself with a wry sigh, if I could somehow fail to notice these things. "I'll start in the bathroom," she says discreetly. "Sir," he reminds her. "Sir," she says.

And she enters. Deliberately and gravely, as though once and for all, without affectation, somewhat encumbered by the vital paraphernalia of her office, yet radiant with that clear-browed self-assurance achieved only by long and generous devotion to duty. She plants her bucket and brushes beside the door, leans the mop and broom against the wall, then crosses the room to fling open (humbly, authoritatively) the curtains and the garden doors: the fragrant air and sunlight come flooding in, a flood she now feels able to appreciate. The sun is already high in the sky, but the garden is still bejeweled with morning dew and (she remembers to notice) there is such a song of birds all about! What inspiration! She enjoys this part of her work: flushing out the stale darkness of the dead night with such grand (yet circumspect) gestures—it's almost an act of magic! Of course, she takes pleasure in *all* her appointed tasks (she reminds herself), whether it be scrubbing floors or polishing furniture or even scouring out the tub or toilet, for she knows that only in giving herself (as he has told her) can she find herself: true service (he doesn't have to tell her!) is perfect freedom. And so, excited by the song of the birds, the sweet breath of morning, and her own natural eagerness to please, she turns with a glad heart to her favorite task of all: the making of the bed. Indeed, all the rest of her work is embraced by it, for the opening up and airing of the bed is the first of her tasks, the making of it her last. Today, however, when she tosses the covers back, she finds, coiled like a dark snake near the foot, a bloodstained leather belt. She starts back. The sheets, too, are flecked with blood. Shadows seem to creep across the room and the birds fall silent. Perhaps, she thinks, her heart sinking, I'd better go out and come in again . . . .

At least, he cautions himself while taking a shower, give her a chance. Her forgetfulness, her clumsiness, her endless comings and goings and stupid mistakes are a trial of course, and he feels sometimes like he's been living with them forever, but she means well and, with patience, instruction, discipline, she can still learn. Indeed, to the extent that she fails, it could be said, *he* has failed. He knows he must be firm, yet understanding, severe if need be, but caring and protective. He vows to treat her today with the civility and kindness due to an inferior, and not to lose his temper, even should she resist. Our passions (he reminds himself) are our infirmities. A sort of fever of the mind, which ever leaves us weaker than it found us. But when he turns off the taps and reaches for the towel, he finds it damp. Again! He can feel the rage rising in him, turning to ash with its uncontrollable heat his gentler intentions. Has she forgotten to change them yet again, he wonders furiously, standing there in a puddle with the cold wet towels clutched in his fists—or has she not even come yet?

She enters once and for all encumbered with her paraphernalia which she deposits by the wall near the door, thinking: it should be easier than this. Indeed, why bother at all when it always seems to turn out the same? Yet she cannot do otherwise. She is driven by a sense of duty and a profound appetite for hope never quite stifled by even the harshest punishments: this time, today, perhaps it will be perfect. . . . So, deliberately and gravely, not staring or turning her head either one way or the other, she crosses the room to the far wall and with a determined flourish draws open the tall curtains, flooding the room with buckets of sunlight, but her mind is clouded with an old obscurity: When, she wants to know as she opens wide the glass doors to let the sweet breath of morning in (there are birds, too, such a song, she doesn't hear it), did all this really begin? When she entered? Before that? Long ago? Not yet? Or just now as, bracing herself as though for some awful trial, she turns upon the bed and flings the covers back, her morning's tasks begun. "Oh!" she cries. "I beg your pardon, sir!" He stares groggily down at the erection poking up out of the fly of his pajama pants, like (she thinks) some kind of luxuriant but dangerous dew-bejeweled blossom: a monster in the garden. "I was having a dream," he announces sleepily, yet gravely. "Something about tumidity. But it kept getting mixed up somehow with—" But she is no longer listening. Watching his knobby plant waggle puckishly in the morning breeze, then dip slowly, wilting toward the shadows like a closing morning glory, a solution of sorts has occurred to her to that riddle of genesis that has been troubling her mind: to wit, that a condition *has* no beginning. Only *change* can begin or end.

She enters, dressed crisply in her black uniform with its starched white apron and lace cap, leans her mop against the wall like a standard, and strides across the gleaming tile floor to fling open the garden doors as though (he thinks) calling forth the morning. What's left of it. Watching her from behind the bathroom door, he is moved by her transparent earnestness, her uncomplicated enthusiasm, her easy self-assurance. What more, really, does he want of her? Never mind that she's forgotten her broom again, or that her shoe's unbuckled and her cap on crooked, or that in her exuberance she nearly broke the glass doors (and sooner or later will), what is wonderful is the quickening of her spirits as she enters, the light that seems to dawn on her face as she opens the room, the way she makes a maid's oppressive routine seem like a sudden invention of love. See now how she tosses back the blankets and strips off the sheets as though, in childish excitement, unwrapping a gift! How in fluffing up the pillows she seems almost to bring them to life! She calls it: "doing the will of God from the heart!" *"Teach me, my God and King, in all things thee to see,"* she sings, *"and what I do in any thing, to do it as for thee!"* Ah well, he envies her: would that he had it so easy! All life is a service, he knows that. To live in the full sense of the word is not to exist or subsist merely, but to make one-self over, to *give* oneself: to some high purpose, to others, to some social end, to life itself beyond the shell of ego. But he, lacking superiors, must devote himself to abstractions, never knowing when he has succeeded, when he has failed, or even if he has the abstractions right, whereas she, needing no others, has him. He would like to explain this to her, to ease the pain of her routine, of her chastisement—what he calls his disciplinary interventions—but he knows that it is he, not she, who is forever in need of such explanations. Her mop fairly flies over the tiles (today she has remembered the mop), making them gleam like mirrors, her face radiant with their reflected light. He checks himself in the bathroom mirror, flicks lint off one shoulder, smoothes the ends of his moustache. If only she could somehow understand how difficult it is for me, he thinks as he steps out to receive her greeting: "Good morning, sir." "Good morning," he replies crisply, glancing around the room. He means to give her some encouragement, to reward her zeal with praise or gratitude or at least a smile to match her own, but instead he finds himself flinging his dirty towels at her feet and snapping: "These towels are damp! See to it that they are replaced!" "Yes, sir!" "Moreover, your apron strings are dangling untidily and there are flyspecks on the mirror!" "Sir." "And another thing!" He strides over to the bed and tears it apart. "Isn't it about time these sheets were changed? Or am I supposed to wear them through before they are taken to be washed?" "But, sir, I just put new–!" "What? *WHAT–?!*" he storms. "Answering back to a reproof? Have you forgotten all I've taught you?" "I–I'm sorry, sir!" "Never answer back if your master takes occasion to reprove you, except–?" "Except it be to acknowledge my fault, sir, and that I am sorry for having committed it, promising to amend for the time to come, and to . . . to . . . ." "Am I being unfair?" he insists, unbuckling his belt. "No, sir," she says, her eyes downcast, shoulders trembling, her arms pressed tight to her sides.

He is strict but not un-kindly. He pays her well, is grateful for her services, treats her respectfully, she doesn't dislike him or even fear him. Nor does she have to work very hard: he is essentially a tidy man, picks up after himself, comes and goes without disturbing things much. A bit of dusting and polishing now and then, fold his pajamas, change the towels, clean the bathroom, scrub the floor, make his bed: really there's nothing to complain about. Yet, vaguely, even as she opens up the garden doors, letting the late morning sunshine and freshness in, she feels unhappy. Not because of what she must do—no, she truly serves with gladness. When she straightens a room, polishes a floor, bleaches a sheet or scrubs a tub, always doing the very best she can, she becomes, she knows, a part of what is good in the world, creating a kind of beauty, revealing a kind of truth. About herself, about life, the things she touches. It's just that, somehow, something is missing. Some response, some enrichment, some direction . . . it's, well, it's too repetitive. Something like that. That's part of the problem anyway. The other part is what she keeps finding in his bed. Things that oughtn't to be there, like old razor blades, broken bottles, banana skins, bloody pessaries, crumbs and ants, leather thongs, mirrors, empty books, old toys, dark stains. Once, even, a frog jumped out at her. No matter how much sunlight and fresh air she lets in, there's always this dark little pocket of lingering night which she has to uncover. It can ruin everything, all

her careful preparations. This morning,
however, all she finds is a pair of flannelette drawers. Ah: she recognizes them.
She glances about guiltily, pulls them on
hastily. Lucky the master's in the bathroom, she thinks, patting down her skirt
and apron, or there'd be the devil to pay.

Something about scour-
ing, or scourging, he can't remember, and
a teacher he once had who called his lectures "lechers." The maid is standing over
him, staring down in some astonishment
at his erection. "Oh! I beg your pardon,
sir!" "I was having a dream . . . ," he
explains, trying to bring it back. "Something about a woman. . . ." But by then he
is alone again. He hears her in the bathroom, running water, singing, whipping

the wet towels off the racks and tossing them out the door. Ah well, it's easy for her, she can come and go. He sits up, squinting in the bright light, watching his erection dip back inside his pajamas like a sleeper pulling the blankets over his head (oh yes! to return there!), then dutifully shoves his feet into slippers, stretches, staggers to the open garden doors. The air is fragrant and there's a morning racket of birds and insects, vaguely threatening. Sometimes, as now, scratching himself idly and dragging himself still from the stupor of sleep, he wonders about his calling, how it came to be his, and when it all began: on his coming here? on *her* coming here? before that, in some ancient time beyond recall? And has he chosen it? or has he, like that woman in his dream, showing him something that for some reason enraged him, been "born with it, sir, for your very utility"?

She strives, understanding the futility of it, for perfection. To arrive properly equipped, to cross the room deliberately, circumspectly, without affectation (as he has taught her), to fling open the garden doors and let the sweet breath of morning flow in and chase the night away, to strip and air the bed and, after all her common tasks, her trivial round, to remake it smooth and tight, all the sheets and blankets tucked in neatly at the sides and bottom, the upper sheet and blankets turned down at the head just so far that their fold covers only half the pillows, all topped with the spread, laid to hang evenly at all sides. And today—perhaps at last! She straightens up, wipes her brow, looks around: yes! he'll be so surprised! Everything perfect! Her heart is pounding as the master, dressed for the day, steps out of the bathroom, marches directly over to the bed, hauls back the covers, picks up a pillow, and hits her in the face with it. Now what did he do that for? "And another thing!" he says.

He awakes, feeling sorry for himself (he's not sure why, something he's been dreaming perhaps, or merely the need to wake just by itself: come, day, do your damage!), tears himself painfully from the bed's embrace, sits up, pushes his feet into slippers. He grunts, squinting in the dimness at his watch: she's late. Just as well. He can shower before she gets here. He staggers into the bathroom and drops his pajamas, struggling to recall his dream. Something about a woman in the civil service, which in her ignorance or cupidity, she insisted on calling the "sibyl service." He is relieving himself noisily when the maid comes in. "Oh! I beg your pardon, sir!" "Good morning," he replies crisply, and pulls his pajamas up, but she is gone. He can hear her outside the door, walking quickly back and forth, flinging open the curtains and garden doors, singing to herself as though lifted by the tasks before her. Sometimes he envies her, having him. Her footsteps carry her to the bed and he hears the rush and flutter of sheets and blankets being thrown back. Hears her scream.

He's not unkind, demands no more than is his right, pays her well, and teaches her things like, "All life is a service, a consecration to some high end," and, "If domestic service is to be tolerable, there must be an attitude of habitual deference on the one side and one of sympathetic protection on the other."

"Every state and condition of life has its particular duties," he has taught her. "The duty of a servant is to be obedient, diligent, sober, just, honest, frugal, orderly in her behavior, submissive and respectful toward her master. She must be contented in her station, because it is necessary that some should be above others in this world, and it was the will of the Almighty to place you in a state of servitude." Her soul, in short, is his invention, and she is grateful to him for it. *"Whatever thy hand findeth to do,"* he has admonished, *"do it with all thy might!"* Nevertheless, looking over her shoulder at her striped sit-me-down in the wardrobe mirror, she wishes he might be a little less literal in applying his own maxims: *he's drawn blood!*

He awakes, mumbling something about a dream, a teacher he

once had, some woman, infirmities. "A
sort of fever of the mind," he explains, his
throat phlegmy with sleep. "Yes, sir," she
says, and flings open the curtains and the
garden doors, letting light and air into the
stale bedroom. She takes pleasure in all her
appointed tasks, but enjoys this one most
of all, more so when the master is already
out of bed, for he seems to resent her wak-
ing him like this. Just as he resents her
arriving late, after he's risen. Either way,
sooner or later, she'll have to pay for
it. "It's a beautiful day," she remarks
hopefully. He sits up with an ambiguous
grunt, rubs his eyes, yawns, shudders.
"You may speak when spoken to," he
grumbles, tucking his closing morning
glory back inside his pajamas (behind her,
bees are humming in the garden and
there's a crackly pulsing of insects, but the
birds have fallen silent: she had thought
today might be perfect, but already it is
slipping away from her), "unless it be to
deliver a message or ask a necessary ques-

tion." "Yes, sir." He shoves his feet into slippers and staggers off to the bathroom, leaving her to face (she expects the worst)–shadows have invaded the room– the rumpled bed alone.

It's not just the damp towels. It's also the streaked floor, the careless banging of the garden doors, her bedraggled uniform, the wrinkled sheets, the confusion of her mind. He lectures her patiently on the proper way to make a bed, the airing of the blankets, turning of the mattress, changing of the sheets, the importance of a smooth surface. "Like a blank sheet of crisp new paper," he tells her. He shows her how to make the correct diagonal creases at the corners, how to fold the top edge of the upper sheet back over the blankets, how to carry the spread under and then over the pillows. Oh, not for his benefit and advantage—he could sleep anywhere or for that matter (in extremity) could make his own bed—but for hers. How else would she ever be able to realize what is best in herself? "A little arrangement and thought will give you method and habit," he explains (it is his "two fairies" lecture), but though she seems willing enough, is polite and deferential, even eager to please, she can never seem to get it just right. Is it a weakness on her part, he wonders as he watches her place the pillows on the bed upsidedown, then tug so hard on the bottom blanket that it comes out at the foot, or some perversity? Is she testing him? She refits the bottom blanket, tucks it in again, but he knows the sheet beneath is now wrinkled. He sighs, removes his belt. Perfection is elusive, but what else is there worth striving for? "Am I being unfair?" he insists.

He's standing there in the sunlight in his slippers and pajama bottoms, cracking his palm with a leather strap, when she enters (once and for all) with all her paraphernalia. She plants the bucket and brushes beside the door, leans the mop and broom against the wall, stacks the fresh linens and towels on a chair. She is late—the curtains and doors are open, her circumspect crossing of the room no longer required—but she remains hopeful. Running his maxims over in her head, she checks off her rags and brushes, her polishes, cleaning powders, razor blades, toilet paper, dustpans—oh no . . . ! Her heart sinks like soap in a bucket. The soap she has forgotten to bring. She sighs, then deliberately and gravely, without affectation, not stamping too loud, nor dragging her legs after her, not marching as if leading a dance, nor keeping time with her head and hands, nor staring or turning her head either one way or the other, she advances sedately and discreetly across the gleaming tiles to the bed, and tucking up her dress and apron, pulling down her flannelette drawers, bends over the foot of it, exposing her soul's ingress to the sweet breath of morning, blowing in from the garden. "I wonder if you can appreciate," he says, picking a bit of lint off his target before applying his corrective measures to it, "how difficult this is for me?"

He awakes, vaguely frightened by something he's dreamt (it was about order or odor and a changed condition— but how did it begin . . . ?), wound up in damp sheets and unable at first even to move, defenseless against the day already hard upon him. Its glare blinds him, but he can hear the maid moving about the room, sweeping the floor, changing the towels, running water, pushing furniture around. "Good morning, sir," she says. "Come here a moment," he replies gruffly, then clears his throat. "Sir?" "Look under the bed. Tell me what you see." He expects the worst: blood, a decapitated head, a bottomless hole . . . "I'm–I'm sorry, sir," she says, tucking up her skirt and apron, lowering her drawers, "I thought I *had* swept it . . . ."

No matter how much fresh air and sunlight she lets in, there is always this little pocket of lingering night which she has to uncover. Once she found a dried bull's pizzle in there, another time a dead mouse in a trap. Even the nice things she finds in the bed are somehow horrible: the toys broken, the food moldy, the clothing torn and bloody. She knows she must always be circumspect and self-effacing, never letting her countenance betray the least dislike toward any task, however trivial or distasteful, and she resolves every morning to be cheerful and good-natured, letting nothing she finds there put her out of temper with everything besides, but sometimes she cannot help herself. "Oh, teach me, my God and King, in all things thee to see, and what I do in any thing, to do it as for thee," she tells herself, seeking courage, and flings back the sheets and blankets. She screams. But it's only money, a little pile of gold coins, agleam with promise. Or challenge: is he testing her?

Oh well, he envies her, even as that seat chosen by Mother Nature for such interventions quivers and reddens under the whistling strokes of the birch rod in his hand. "Again!" "Be . . . be diligent in endeavoring to please your master—be faithful and . . . and . . ." Swish-*SNAP!* "Oh, sir!" "Honest!" "Yes, sir!" She, after all, is free to come and go, her correction finitely inscribed by time and the manuals, but he . . . He sighs unhappily. How did it all begin, he wonders. Was it destiny, choice, generosity? If she would only get it right for once, he reasons, bringing his stout engine of duty down with a sharp report on her brightly striped but seemingly unimpressionable hinder parts, he might at least have time for a stroll in the garden. Does she—*CRACK!*—think he enjoys this? "Well?" "Be . . . be faithful, honest and submissive to him, sir, and—" Whish-*SLASH!* "And—*gasp!*—do not incline to be slothful! Or—" *THWOCK!* "Ow! Please, sir!" Hiss-*WHAP!* She groans, quivers, starts. The two raised hemispheres upon which the blows from the birch rod have fallen begin (predictably) to make involuntary motions both vertically and horizontally, the constrictor muscle being hard at work, the thighs also participating in the general vibrations, all in all a dismal spectacle. And for nothing? So it would seem . . . "Or?" "Or lie long in bed, sir, but rise . . . rise early in a morning!" The weals criss-cross each other on her enflamed posteriors like branches against the pink clouds of dawn, which for some reason saddens him. "Am I being unfair?" "No—no, s—" Whisp-*CRACK!* She shows no tears, but her face pressed against the bedding is flushed, her lips trembling, and she breathes heavily as though she's been running, confirming the quality of the rod which is his own construction. "Sir," he reminds her, turning away. "Sir," she replies faintly. "Thank you, sir."

She enters, once and for all, radiant and clear-browed (a long devotion to duty), with all her paraphernalia, her mop and bucket, brooms, rags, soaps, polishes, sets them all down, counting them off on her fingers, then crosses the room deliberately and circumspectly, not glancing at the rumpled bed, and flings open the curtains and the garden doors to call forth the morning, what's left of it. There is such a song of insects all about (the preying birds are silent) – what inspiration! "Lord, keep me in my place!" The master is in the shower: she hears the water. "Let me be diligent in performing whatever my master commands me," she prays, "neat and clean in my habit, modest in my carriage, silent when he is angry, willing to please, quick and neat-handed about what I do, and always of an humble and good disposition!" Then, excited to the most generous and efficient accomplishments, she turns with a palpitating heart (she is thinking about perfect service and freedom and the unpleasant

things she has found) to the opening up
and airing of the bed. She braces herself,
expecting the worst, but finds only a
wilted flower from the garden: ah! today
then! she thinks hopefully–perhaps at
last! But then she hears the master turn
the taps off, step out of the shower. Oh no
. . . ! She lowers her drawers to her knees,
lifts her dress, and bends over the unmade
bed. *"These towels are damp!"* he blusters,
storming out of the bathroom, wielding
the fearsome rod, that stout engine of
duty, still wet from the shower.

Sometimes he uses a rod,
sometimes his hand, his belt, sometimes a
whip, a cane, a cat-o'-nine-tails, a bull's
pizzle, a hickory switch, a martinet, ruler,
slipper, a leather strap, a hairbrush. There
are manuals for this. Different prepara-

tions and positions to be assumed, the number and severity of the strokes gener- ally prescribed to fit the offense, he has explained it all to her, though it is not what is important to her. She knows he is just, could not be otherwise if he tried, even if the relative seriousness of the vari- ous infractions seems somewhat obscure to her at times. No, what matters to her is the idea behind the regulations that her daily tasks, however trivial, are perfectible. Not absolutely perhaps, but at least in terms of the manuals. This idea, which is almost tangible—made manifest, as it were, in the weals on her behind—is what the punishment is for, she assumes. She does not enjoy it certainly, nor (she be- lieves—and it wouldn't matter if he did) does he. Rather, it is a road (speaking loosely), the rod, to bring her daily nearer God—and what's more, it seems that she's succeeding at last! Today everything has been perfect: her entry, all her vital paraphernalia, her circumspect crossing of the room and opening of the garden doors, her scrubbing and waxing and dusting and polishing, her opening up and airing and making of the master's bed—everything! True service, she knows (he has taught her!), is perfect freedom, and today she feels it: almost like a breeze—the sweet breath of success—lifting her! But then the master emerges from the bathroom, his hair wild, fumbles through the clothes hanging in the wardrobe, pokes through the dresser drawers, whips back the covers of her perfectly made bed. "What's this doing here—?!" he demands, holding up his comb. "I—I'm sorry, sir! It wasn't there when I—" "What? *What—?!*" He seizes her by the elbow, drags her to the foot of the bed, forces her to bend over it. "I have been very indulgent to you up to now, but now I am going to punish you severely, to cure you of your insolent clumsiness once and for all! So pull up your skirt—come! pull it up! you know well enough that the least show of resistance means ten extra cuts of the—*what's this—?!*" She peers round her shoulder at her elevated sit-me-down, so sad and pale above her stockings. "I—I don't understand, sir! I had them on when I came in—!"

Perhaps he's been pushing her too hard, he muses, soaping himself in the shower and trying to recall the dream he was having when she woke him up (something about ledgers and manual positions, a woman, and the merciless invention of souls which was a sort of fever of the mind), perhaps he's been expecting too much too soon, making her overanxious, for in some particulars now she is almost too efficient, clattering in with her paraphernalia like a soldier, blinding him with a sudden brutal flood of sunlight from the garden, hauling the sheets out from under him while he's still trying to stuff his feet into his slippers. Perhaps he should back off a bit, give her a chance to recover some of her ease and spontaneity, even at the expense of a few undisciplined errors. Perhaps . . . yet he knows he could never let up, even if he tried. Not that he enjoys all this punishment, any more (he assumes, but it doesn't matter) than she does. No, he would rather do just about anything else—crawl back into bed, read his manuals, even take a stroll in the garden—but he is committed to a higher end, his life a mission of sorts, a consecration, and so punish her he must, for to the extent that she fails, he fails. As he turns off the taps and steps out of the shower, reaching for the towel, the maid rushes in. "Oh, I beg your pardon, sir!" He grabs a towel and wraps it around him, but she snatches it away again: "That one's damp, sir!" She dashes out to fetch him a fresh one and he is moved by her transparent enthusiasm, her eagerness to please, her seemingly unquenchable appetite for hope: perhaps today . . . ! But he has already noticed that she has forgotten her lace cap, there's a dark stain on the bib of her apron, and her garters are dangling. He sighs, reaches for the leather strap. Somehow (is there to be no end to this? he wonders ruefully) it should be easier than this.

She does not enjoy the discipline of the rod, nor does he—or so he believes, though what would it matter if he did? Rather, they are both dedicated to the fundamental proposition (she winces at the painful but unintended pun, while peering over her shoulder at herself in the wardrobe mirror, tracing the weals with her fingertips) that her daily tasks, however trivial, are perfectible, her punishments serving her as a road, loosely speaking, to bring her daily nearer God, at least in terms of the manuals. Tenderly, she lifts her drawers up over her blistered sit-me-down, smoothes down her black alpaca dress and white lace apron, wipes the tears from her eyes, and turns once more to the unmade bed. Outside, the bees humming in the noonday sun remind her of all the time she's lost. At least, she consoles herself, the worst is past. But the master is pacing the room impatiently and she's fearful his restlessness will confuse her again. "Why don't you go for a stroll in the garden, sir?" she suggests deferentially. "You may speak when spoken to!" he reminds her, jabbing a finger at her sharply. "I–I'm sorry, sir!" "You must be careful not only to do your work quietly, but to keep out of sight as much as possible, and never begin to speak to your master unless—?" "Unless it be to deliver a message, sir, or ask a necessary question!" "And then to do it in as few words as possible," he adds, getting down his riding whip. "Am I being unfair?" "But, sir! you've already—!" "What? *What—?!* Answering back to a reproof—?" "But—!" *"Enough!"* he rages, seizing her by the arm and dragging her over to the bed. *"Please—!"*But he pulls her down over his left knee, pushes her head down on the stripped mattress, locking her legs in place with his right leg, clamps her right wrist in the small of her back, throws her skirts back and jerks her drawers down. *"Oh, sir—!"* she pleads, what is now her highest part still radiant and throbbing from the previous lesson. "SILENCE!" he roars, lifting the whip high above his head, a curious strained expression on his face. She can hear the whip sing as he brings it down, her cheeks pinch together involuntarily, her heart leaps—*"he'll draw blood!"*

Where does she come from? Where does she go? He doesn't know. All he knows is that every day she comes here, dressed in her uniform and carrying all her paraphernalia with her, which she sets down by the door; then she crosses the room, opens up the curtains and garden doors, makes his bed soft and easy, first airing the bedding, turning the mattress, and changing the linens, scrubs and waxes the tiled floor, cleans the bath-room, polishes the furniture and all the mirrors, replenishes all supplies, and somewhere along the way commits some fundamental blunder, obliging him to administer the proper correction. Every day the same. Why does he persist? It's not so

much that he shares her appetite for hope
(though sometimes, late in the day, he
does), but that he could not do otherwise
should he wish. To live in the full sense of
the word, he knows, is not merely to exist,
but to give oneself to some mission, sur-
render to a higher purpose, but in truth he
often wonders, watching that broad part
destined by Mother Nature for such solemnities quiver and redden under his
hand (he thinks of it as a blank ledger on
which to write), whether it is he who has
given himself to a higher end, or that end
which has chosen and in effect captured
him?

Perhaps, she thinks, I'd
better go out and come in again. . . . And
so she enters. As though once and for all,
though she's aware she can never be sure

of this. She sets down beside the door all the vital paraphernalia of her office, checking off each item on her fingers, then crosses the room (circumspectly etc.) and flings open the curtains and garden doors to the midday sun. Such a silence all about? She tries to take heart from it, but it is not so inspiring as the song of birds, and even the bees seem to have ceased their humming. Though she has resolved, as always, to be cheerful and goodnatured, truly serving with gladness as she does, she nevertheless finds her will flagging, her mind clouded with old obscurities: somehow, something is missing. "Teach me, my God and King, in all things thee to see," she recites dutifully, but the words seem meaningless to her and go nowhere. And now, once again, the hard part. She holds back, trembling—but what can she do about it? For she knows her place and is contented with her station, as he has taught her. She takes a deep breath of the clean warm air blowing in from the garden and, fearing the worst, turns upon the bed, hurls the covers back, and screams. But it is only the master. "Oh! I beg your pardon, sir!" "A . . . a dream," he explains huskily, as his erection withdraws into his pajamas like a worm caught out in the sun, burrowing for shade. "Something about a lecture on civil severity, what's left of it, and an inventory of soaps . . . or hopes . . ." He's often like that as he struggles (never very willingly, it seems to her) out of sleep. She leaves him there, sitting on the edge of the bed, squinting in the bright light, yawning and scratching himself and muttering something depressing about being born again, and goes to the bathroom to change the towels, check the toothpaste and toilet paper, wipe the mirror and toilet seat, and put fresh soap in the shower tray, doing the will of God and the manuals, endeavoring to please. As he shuffles groggily in, al-

ready reaching inside his fly, she slips out,
careful not to speak as she's not been spoken to, and returns to the rumpled bed.
She tosses back the blankets afresh (nothing new, thank you, sir), strips away the
soiled linens, turns and brushes the mattress (else it might imbibe an unhealthy
kind of dampness and become unpleasant), shakes the feather pillows and sets
everything out to air. While the master
showers, she dusts the furniture, polishes
the mirrors, and mops the floor, then remakes the bed, smooth and tight, all the
sheets and blankets tucked in neatly at the
sides and bottom, the top sheet turned
down at the head, over the blankets, the
spread carried under, then over the pillows, and hanging equally low at both
sides and the foot: ah! it's almost an act of
magic! But are those flyspecks on the mirror? She rubs the mirror, and seeing herself reflected there, thinks to check that
her apron strings are tied and her stocking

seams are straight. Peering over her shoulder at herself, her eye falls on the mirrored bed: one of the sheets is dangling at the foot, peeking out from under the spread as though exposing itself rudely. She hurries over, tucks it in, being careful to make the proper diagonal fold, but now the spread seems to be hanging lower on one side than the other. She whips it back, dragging the top sheet and blankets part way with it. The taps have been turned off, the master is drying himself. Carefully, she remakes the bed, tucking in all the sheets and blankets properly, fluffing the pillows up once more, covering it all with the spread, hung evenly. All this bedmaking has raised a lot of dust: she can see her own tracks on the floor. Hurriedly she wipes the furniture again and sweeps the tiles. Has she bumped the bed somehow? The spread is askew once again like a gift coming unwrapped. She tugs it to one side, sees ripples appear on top. She tries to smooth them down, but apparently the blankets are wrinkled underneath. She hasn't pushed the dresser back against the wall. The wardrobe door is open, reflecting the master standing in the doorway to the bathroom, slapping his palm with a bull's pizzle. She stands there, downcast, shoulders trembling, her arms pressed to her sides, unable to move. It's like some kind of failure of communication, she thinks, her diligent endeavors to please him forever thwarted by her irremediable clumsiness. "Come, come! A little arrangement and thought will give you method and habit," he reminds her gravely, "two fairies that will make the work disappear before a ready pair of hands!" In her mind she doesn't quite believe it, but her heart is ever hopeful, her hands readier than he knows. She takes the bed apart once more and remakes it from the beginning, tucking everything in correctly, fluffing the pillows, laying the spread evenly: all tight and smooth it looks. Yes! She pushes the dresser (once he horsed her there: she shudders to recall it, a flush of dread racing through her) back against the wall, collects the wet towels he has thrown on the floor, closes the wardrobe door. In the mirror, she sees the bed. The spread and blankets have been thrown back, the sheets pulled out. In the bathroom doorway, the master taps his palm with the stretched-out bull's pizzle, testing its firmness and elasticity, which she knows to be terrifying in its perfection. She remakes the bed tight and smooth, not knowing what else to do, vaguely aware as she finishes of an unpleasant odor. Under the bed? Also her apron is missing and she seems to have a sheet left over. Shadows creep across the room, silent now but for the rhythmic tapping of the pizzle in the master's hand and the pounding of her own palpitating heart.

Sometimes he stretches her across his lap. Sometimes she must bend over a chair or the bed, or lie flat out on it, or be horsed over the pillows, the dresser or a stool, there are manuals for this. Likewise her drawers: whether they are to be drawn tight over her buttocks like a second skin or lowered, and if lowered, by which of them, how far, and so on. Her responses are assumed in the texts (the writhing, sobbing, convulsive quivering, blushing, moaning, etc.), but not specified, except insofar as they determine his own further reactions—to resistance, for example, or premature acquiescence, fainting, improper language, an unclean bottom, and the like. Thus, once again, her relative freedom: her striped buttocks tremble and dance spontaneously under the whip which his hand must bring whistling down on them according to canon—ah well, it's not so

much that he envies her (her small free-
doms cost her something, he knows that),
but that he is saddened by her inability to
understand how difficult it is for him, and
without that understanding it's as though
something is always missing, no matter
how faithfully he adheres to the regulations. "And–?" "And be neat and clean in
your–" whisp-*CRACK!* "–OW! habit!
Oh! and wash yourself all over once a day
to avoid bad smells and–" hiss-*SNAP!*
"–and–*gasp!*–wear strong decent under-
clothing!" The whip sings a final time,
smacks its broad target with a loud report,
and little drops of blood appear like punc-
tuation, gratitude, morning dew. "That
will do, then. See that you don't forget to
wear them again!" "Yes, sir." She lowers
her black alpaca skirt gingerly over the
glowing crimson flesh as though hooding
a lamp, wincing at each touch. "Thank
you, sir."

For a long time she struggled to perform her tasks in such a way as to avoid the thrashings. But now, with time, she has come to understand that the tasks, truly common, are only peripheral details in some larger scheme of things which includes her punishment—indeed, perhaps depends upon it. Of course she still performs her duties *as though* they were perfectible and her punishment could be avoided, ever diligent in endeavoring to please him who guides her, but though each day the pain surprises her afresh, the singing of the descending instrument does not. That God has ordained bodily punishment (and Mother Nature designed the proper place of martyrdom) is beyond doubt—every animal is governed by it, understands and fears it, and the fear of it keeps every creature in its own sphere, forever preventing (as he has taught her) that natural confusion and disorder that would instantly arise without it. Every state and condition of life has its particular duties, and each is subject to the divine government of pain, nothing could be more obvious, and looked on this way, his chastisements are not merely necessary, they might even be beautiful. Or so she consoles herself, trying to take heart, calm her rising panic, as she crosses the room under his stern implacable gaze, lowers her drawers as far as her knees, tucks her skirt up, and bends over the back of a chair, hands on the seat, thighs taut and pressed closely together, what is now her highest part tensing involuntarily as though to reduce the area of pain, if not the severity. "It's . . . it's a beautiful day, sir," she says hopefully. "What? *WHAT–?!*"

    Relieving himself noisily in the bathroom, the maid's daily recitals in the next room (such a blast of light out there–even in here he keeps his eyes half closed) thus drowned out, he wonders if there's any point in going on. She is late, has left half her paraphernalia behind, is improperly dressed, and he knows, even without looking, that the towels are damp. Maybe it's some kind of failure of communication. A mutual failure. Is that possible? A loss of syntax between stroke and weal? No, no, even if possible, it is unthinkable. He turns on the shower taps and lets fall his pajama pants, just as the maid comes in with a dead fetus and drops it down the toilet, flushes it. "I found it in your bed, sir," she explains gratuitously (is she testing him?), snatching up the damp towels, but failing to replace them with fresh ones. At least she's remembered her drawers today: she's wearing them around her ankles. He sighs as she shuffles out. Maybe he should simply forget it, go for a stroll in the gar-

den or something, crawl back into bed (a
dream, he recalls now: something about
lectures or ledgers—an inventory perhaps—and a bottomless hole, glass break-
ing, a woman doing what she called "the
hard part" . . . or did she say "heart
part"?), but of course he cannot, even if
he truly wished to. He is not a free man,
his life is consecrated, for though he is *her*
master, her failures are inescapably *his*. He
turns off the shower taps, pulls up his pajama pants, takes down the six-thonged
martinet. "I have been very indulgent to
you up to now," he announces, stepping
out of the bathroom, "but now I am
going to punish you severely, so pull up
your skirt, come! pull it up!" But, alas, it
is already up. She is bent over the foot of
the bed, her pale hinder parts already exposed for his ministrations, an act of inso-
lence not precisely covered by his manuals. Well, he reasons wryly, making the
martinet sing whole chords, if improvisa-

tion is denied him, interpretation is not. "Ow, sir! Please! *You'll draw blood, sir!*"

Neat and clean in habit, modest—" *WHACK!* "—in . . . in carriage, silent when—" Whisp-*SNAP!* "OW!!" "Be careful! If you move, the earlier blow won't count!" "I—I'm sorry, sir!" Her soul, she knows, is his invention, and she is grateful to him for it, but exposed like this to the whining slashes of the cane and the sweet breath of mid-afternoon which should cool his righteous ardor but doesn't (once a bee flew in and stung him on the hand: what did it mean? nothing: she got it on her sit-me-down once, too, and he took the swelling for a target), her thighs shackled by flannelette drawers and blood rushing to her head, she can never remember (for all the times he has ex-

plained it to her) why it is that Mother
Nature has chosen that particular part of
her for such solemnities: it seems more
like a place for lettings things out than
putting things in. "Well? Silent when–?"
"Silent when he is angry, willing to please,
quick and–" swish-*CRACK!* "–and of
good disposition!" "Sir," he reminds her:
THWOCK! "SIR!" she cries. "Very well,
but you must learn to take more pleasure
in your appointed tasks, however trivial or
unpleasant, and when you are ordered to
do anything, do not grumble or let your
countenance betray any dislike thereunto,
but do it cheerfully and readily!" "Yes, sir!
Thank you, sir!" She is all hot behind, and
peering over her shoulder at herself in the
wardrobe mirror after the master has gone
to shower, she can see through her tears
that it's like on fire, flaming crimson it is,
with large blistery welts rising and throbbing like things alive: he's drawn blood!
She dabs at it with her drawers, recalling a

dream he once related to her about a teacher he'd had who called his chastisements "scripture lessons," and she understands now what he's always meant by demanding "a clean sheet of paper." Well, certainly it has always been clean, neat and clean as he's taught her, that's one thing she's never got wrong, always washing it well every day in three hot lathers, letting the last lather be made thin of the soap, then not rinsing it or toweling it, but drying it over brimstone, keeping it as much from the air as possible, for that, she knows, will spoil it if it comes to it. She finishes drying it by slapping it together in her hands, then holding it before a good fire until it be thoroughly hot, then clapping it and rubbing it between her hands from the fire, occasionally adding to its fairness by giving it a final wash in a liquor made of rosemary flowers boiled in white wine. Now, she reasons, lifting her drawers up gingerly over the hot tender flesh,

which is still twitching convulsively, if
she could just apply those same two fairies, method and habit, to the rest of her
appointed tasks, she might yet find in
them that pleasure he insists she take, according to the manuals. Well, anyway, the
worst is past. Or so she consoles herself,
as smoothing down her black skirt and
white lace apron, she turns to the bed.
*"Oh, teach me, my God and King, in all
things thee to . . ."* What—? There's something under there! *And it's moving . . . !*

"Thank you, sir." "I
know that perfection is elusive," he explains, putting away his stout engine of
duty, while she staggers over, her knees
bound by her drawers, to examine her
backside in the wardrobe mirror (it is well
cut, he knows, and so aglow one might

cook little birds over it or roast chestnuts, as the manuals suggest), "but what else is there worth striving for?" "Yes, sir." She shows no tears, but her face is flushed, her lips are trembling, and she breathes as though she has been running. He goes to gaze out into the garden, vaguely dissatisfied. The room is clean, the bed stripped and made, the maid whipped, why isn't that enough? Is there something missing in the manuals? No, more likely, he has failed somehow to read them rightly. Yet again. Outside in the sleepy afternoon heat of the garden, the bees are humming, insects chattering, gentler sounds to be sure than the hiss of a birch rod, the sharp report as it smacks firm resonant flesh, yet strangely alien to him, sounds of natural confusion and disorder from a world without precept or invention. He sighs. Though he was thinking "invention," what he has heard in his inner ear was "intention," and now he's not sure which it was he truly meant. Perhaps he should back off a bit—or even let her off altogether for a few days. A kind of holiday from the divine government of pain. Certainly he does not enjoy it nor (presumably) does she. If he could ever believe in her as she believes in him, he might even change places with her for awhile, just to ease his own burden and let her understand how difficult it is for him. A preposterous idea of course, pernicious in fact, an unthinkable betrayal . . . yet sometimes, late in the day, something almost like a kind of fever of the mind (speaking loosely) steals over—enough! *enough!* no shrinking! "And another thing!" he shouts, turning on the bed (she is at the door, gathering up her paraphernalia) and throwing back the covers: at the foot on the clean crisp sheets there is a little pile of wriggling worms, still coated with dirt from the garden. "WHAT DOES THIS MEAN—?!" he screams. "I— I'm sorry, sir! I'll clean it up right away, sir!" Is she testing him? Taunting him? It's almost an act of madness! "Am I being unfair?" "But, sir, you've already–!" "What? *WHAT–?!* Is there to be no *end* to this–?!"

He holds her over his left knee, her legs locked between his, wrist clamped in the small of her back, her skirt up and her drawers down, and slaps her with his bare hand, first one buttock, reddening it smartly in contrast to the dazzling alabaster (remembering the manuals) of the other, then attacking its companion with equal alacrity. "Ow! Please, sir!" "Come, come, you know that the least show of resistance means ten extra cuts of the rod!" he admonishes her, doubling her over a chair. "When you are ordered to do anything, do not grumble or let your countenance betray any dislike thereunto, but do it cheerfully and generously!" "Yes, sir, but—" "What? *WHAT—?!*" Whish-*CRACK!* "OW!" *SLASH!* Her crimson bottom, hugged close to the pillows, bobs and dances under the whistling cane. "When anyone finds fault with you, do not answer rudely!" Whirr-*SMACK!* "NO, SIR!" Each stroke, surprising her afresh, makes her jerk with pain and wrings a little cry from her (as anticipated by the manuals when the bull's pizzle is employed), which she attempts to stifle by burying her face in the horsehair cushion. "Be respectful—?" "Be respectful and obedient, sir, to those—" swish-*THWOCK!* "—placed—OW!—placed OVER you— AARGH!" Whizz-*SWACK!* "With fear and trembling—" *SMASH!* "—and in singleness of your heart!" he reminds her gravely as she groans, starts, quivers under his patient instruction. "Ouch! Yes, sir!" The leather strap whistles down to land with a loud crack across the center of her glowing buttocks, seeming almost to explode, and making what lilies there are left into roses. *SMACK!* Ker-*WHACK!* He's working well now. "Am I being unfair?" "N-no, sir!" *WHAP! SLAP!* Horsed over the dresser her limbs launch out helplessly with each blow, *"Kneel down!"* She falls humbly to her hands and knees, her head bowed between his slippered feet, that broad part destined by Mother Nature for such devotions elevated but pointed away from him toward the wardrobe mirror (as though trying, flushed and puffed up, to cry out to itself), giving him full and immediate access to that large division referred to in the texts as the Paphian grove. "And resolve every morning—?" "Resolve—*gasp!*—resolve every morning to be cheerful and—" He raises the whip, snaps it three times around his head, and brings it down with a crash on her hinder parts, driving her head forward between his legs.

"And– *YOW!*–and good-natured that . . . that day, and if any . . . if any accident– *groan!*–should happen to–" swish– *WHACK!*"–to break that resolution, suffer it . . . suffer it not–" *SLASH!* "Oh, sir!" *SWOCK!* He's pushing himself, too, hard perhaps, but he can't– "Please, sir! *PLEASE!*" She is clinging to his knee, sobbing into his pajama pants, the two raised hemispheres upon which the strokes have fallen making involuntary motions both vertically and horizontally as though sending a message of distress, all the skin wrinkling like the surface of a lake rippled by the wind. "What are you doing?! *WHAT DOES THIS MEAN–?!*" He spanks her with a hairbrush, lashes her with a cat-o'-nine-tails, flagellates her with nettles, not shrinking from the hard service to be done, this divine drudgery, clear-browed in his devotion to duty. Perhaps today . . . ! "SIR!" He pauses, breathing heavily. His arm hurts. There is a curious strained expression on her face, flushed like her behind and wet with tears. "Sir, if you . . . if you don't stop—" "What? *WHAT—?!*" "You—you won't know what to do *next!*" "Ah." He has just been smacking her with a wet towel, and the damp rush and pop, still echoing in his inner ear, reminds him dimly of a dream, perhaps the one she interrupted when she arrived. In it there was something about humidity, but it kept getting mixed up somehow with hymnody, such that every time she opened her mouth (there was a woman in the dream) damp chords flowed out and stained his ledgers, bleached white as clean sheets. "I'm so old," he says, letting his arm drop, "and still each day . . ." "Sir?" "Nothing. A dream . . ." Where was he? It doesn't matter. "Why don't you go for a stroll in the garden, sir? It's a beautiful day." Such impudence: he ignores it. "It's all right," he says, draping the blood-flecked towel over his shoulder, scratching himself idly. He yawns. "The worst is past."

Has he devoted himself to a higher end, he wonders, standing there in the afternoon sunlight in his slippers and pajama bottoms, flexing a cane, testing it, snapping it against his palm, or has he been taken captive by it? Is choice itself an illusion? Or an act of magic? And *is* the worst over, or has it not yet begun? He shudders, yawns, stretches. And the manuals . . . ? He is afraid even to ask, takes a few practice strokes with the cane against a horsehair cushion instead. When the riddles and paradoxes of his calling overtake him, wrapping him in momentary darkness, he takes refuge in the purity of technique. The proper stretching of a

bull's pizzle, for example, this can occupy
him for hours. Or the fabrication of whipping chairs, the index of duties and of-
fenses, the synonymy associated with cor-
poral discipline and with that broad part
destined by Mother Nature for such services. And a cane is not simply any cane,
but preferably one made like this one of
brown Malacca—the stem of an East In-
dian rattan palm—about two and a half
feet long (give or take an inch and a half)
and a quarter of an inch thick. Whing-
SNAP! listen to it! Or take the birch rod,
not a mere random handful of birchen
twigs, as often supposed, but an instrument of precise and elaborate construction. First, the twigs must be meticulously
selected for strength and elasticity, each
about two feet long, full of snap and taken
from a young tree, the tips sharp as
needles. Then carefully combining the
thick with the thin and slender, they must

be bound together for half their length, tightly enough that they might enjoy long service, yet not too tightly or else the rod will be like a stick and the twigs have no play. The rod must fit conveniently to the hand, have reach and swing so as to sing in the air, the larger part of all punishment being the anticipation of course, not the pain, and must immediately raise welts and blisters, surprising the chastised flesh afresh with each stroke. To be sure, it is easier to construct a birch rod than to employ it correctly–that's always the hard part, he doesn't enjoy it, nor does she surely, but the art of the rod is incomplete without its perfect application. And though elusive, what else is there worth striving for? Indeed, he knows he has been too indulgent toward her up till now, treating her with the civility and kindness due to an inferior, but forgetting the forging of her soul by way of those "vivid lessons," as a teacher he once had used to put it, "in holy scripture, hotly writ." So when she arrives, staggering in late with all her paraphernalia, her bucket empty and her bib hanging down, he orders her straight to the foot of the bed. "But, sir, I haven't even—" "Come, come, no dallying! The least show of resistance will double the punishment! Up with your skirt, up, up! for I intend to— WHAT?! IS THERE TO BE NO END TO THIS—?!" "I—I'm sorry! I was wearing them when I came—I must have left them somewhere . . . !" Maybe it's some kind of communication problem, he thinks, staring gloomily at her soul's ingress which confronts him like blank paper, laundered tiffany, a perversely empty ledger. The warm afternoon sun blows in through the garden doors, sapping his brave resolve. He feels himself drifting, yawning, must literally shake himself to

bring the manuals back to mind, his duties, his devotion . . . "Sir," she reminds
him. "Sir," he sighs.

It never ends. Making
the bed, she scatters dust and feathers
afresh or tips over the mop bucket. Cleaning up the floor, she somehow disturbs
the bed. Or something does. It's almost as
if it were alive. Blankets wrinkle, sheets
peek perversely out from under the spread,
pillows seem to sag or puff up all by them-
selves if she turns her back, and if she
doesn't, then flyspecks break out on the
mirror behind her like pimples, towels
start to drip, stains appear on her apron. If
she hasn't forgotten it. She sighs, turns
once more on the perfidious bed. Though
always of an humble and good disposition
(as she's been taught), diligent in endeav-

oring to please him, and grateful for the opportunity to do the will of God from the heart by serving him (true service, perfect freedom, she knows all about that), sometimes, late in the day like this (shadows are creeping across the room and in the garden the birds are beginning to sing again), she finds herself wishing she could make the bed once and for all: glue down the sheets, sew on the pillows, stiffen the blankets as hard as boards and nail them into place. But then what? She cannot imagine. Something frightening. No, no, better this trivial round, these common tasks, and a few welts on her humble sit-me-down, she reasons, tucking the top sheet and blankets in neatly at the sides and bottom, turning them down at the head just so far that their fold covers half the pillows, than be overtaken by confusion and disorder. *"Teach me, my God and King,"* she sings out hopefully, floating the spread out over the bed, allowing it to fall evenly on all sides, *"in all things thee to—"* But then, as the master steps out of the bathroom behind her, she sees the blatant handprints on the wardrobe mirror, the streamers of her lace cap peeking out from under the dresser, standing askew. "I'm sorry, sir," she says, bending over the foot of the bed, presenting to him that broad part destined by Mother Nature for the arduous invention of souls. But he ignores it. Instead he tears open the freshly made bed, crawls into it fully dressed, kicking her in the face through the blankets with his shoes, pulls the sheets over his head, and commences to snore. Perhaps, she thinks, her heart sinking, I'd better go out and come in again . . . .

Perhaps I should go for a stroll in the garden, he muses, dutifully reddening one resonant cheek with a firm volley of slaps, then the other, according to the manuals. I'm so old, and still . . . He sighs ruefully, recalling a dream he was having when the maid arrived (when was that?), something about a woman, bloody morning glories (or perhaps in the dream they were "mourning" glories: there was also something about a Paphian grave), and a bee that flew in and stung him on his tumor, which kept getting mixed up somehow with his humor, such that, swollen with pain, he was laughing like a dead man. . . . "Sir?" "What? *WHAT—?!*" he cries, starting up. "Ah . . ." His hand is resting idly on her flushed behind as though he meant to leave it there. "I . . . I was just testing the heat," he explains gruffly, taking up the birch rod, testing it for strength and elasticity to wake his fingers up. "When I'm finished, you'll be able to cook little birds over it or roast chestnuts!" He raises the rod, swings it

three times round his head, and brings it
down with a whirr and a slash, reciting to
himself from the manuals to keep his
mind, clouded with old obscurities, on
the task before him: "Sometimes the oper-
ation is begun a little above the garter—"
whish-*SNAP!* "—and ascending the pearly
inverted cones—" hiss-*WHACK!* "—is carried by degrees to the dimpled promonto-
ries—" *THWOCK!* "—which are vulgarly
called the buttocks!" *SMASH!* "Ow, sir!
PLEASE!" She twists about on his knee,
biting her lip, her highest part flexing and
quivering with each blow, her knees scis-
soring frantically between his legs. "Oh,
teach me," she cries out, trying to stifle
the sobs, "my God and—" whizz-*CRACK!*
"—King, thee—*gasp!*—to—" *WHAP!*
"—SEE!" Sometimes, especially late in the
day like this, watching the weals emerge
from the blank page of her soul's ingress
like secret writing, he finds himself search-
ing it for something, he doesn't know

what exactly, a message of sorts, the reve-
lation of a mystery in the spreading flush,
in the pout and quiver of her cheeks, the
repressed stutter of the little explosions
of wind, the – whush-*SMACK!* – dew-bejeweled hieroglyphs of crosshatched
stripes. But no, the futility of his labors,
that's all there is to read there. Birdsong,
no longer threatening, floats in on the
warm afternoon breeze while he works.
There *was* a bee once, he remembers, that
part of his dream was true. Only it stung
him on his hand, as though to remind
him of the painful burden of his office. For
a long time after that he kept the garden
doors closed altogether, until he realized
one day, spanking the maid for failing to
air the bedding properly, that he was in
some wise interfering with the manuals.
And what has she done wrong today? he
wonders, tracing the bloody welts with
his fingertips. He has forgotten. It doesn't
matter. He can lecture her on those two

fairies, confusion and disorder. Method and habit, rather . . . "Sir . . . ?" "Yes, yes, in a minute . . ." He leans against the bedpost. To live in the full sense of the word, he reminds himself, is not to exist or subsist merely, but to . . . to . . . He yawns. He doesn't remember.

While examining the dismal spectacle of her throbbing sit-me-down in the wardrobe mirror (at least the worst is past, she consoles herself, only half believing it), a solution of sorts to that problem of genesis that's been troubling her occurs to her: to wit, that change (she is thinking about change now, and conditions) is eternal, has no beginning—only conditions can begin or end. Who knows, perhaps he has even taught her that. He has taught her so many things, she can't be sure anymore. Everything from habitual deference and the washing of tiffany to pillow fluffing, true service and perfect freedom, the two fairies that make the work (speaking loosely) disappear, proper carriage, sheet folding, and the divine government of pain. Sometimes, late in the day, or on being awakened, he even tells her about his dreams, which seem to be mostly about lechers and ordure and tumors and bottomless holes (once he said "souls"). In a way it's the worst part of her job (that and the things she finds in the bed: today it was broken glass). Once he told her of a dream about a bird with blood in its beak. She asked him, in all deference, if he was afraid of the garden, whereupon he ripped her drawers down, horsed her over a stool, and flogged her so mercilessly she couldn't stand up after, much less sit down. Now she merely says, "Yes, sir," but that doesn't always temper the vigor of his dis-

ciplinary interventions, as he likes to call
them. Such a one for words and all that!
Tracing the radiant weals on that broad
part of her so destined with her fingertips,
she wishes that just once she might hear
something more like, "Well done, thou
good and faithful servant, depart in
peace!" But then what? When she re-
turned, could it ever be the same? Would
he even want her back? No, no, she thinks
with a faint shudder, lifting her flannelette drawers up gingerly over soul's
well-ruptured ingress (she hopes more has
got in than is leaking out), the sweet
breath of late afternoon blowing in to remind her of the time lost, the work yet
to be done: no, far better her appointed
tasks, her trivial round and daily act of
contrition, no matter how pitiless the
master's interpretation, than conse-
quences so utterly unimaginable. So, in-
spirited by her unquenchable appetite for
hope and clear-browed devotion to duty,

and running his maxims over in her head, she sets about doing the will of God from the heart, scouring the toilet, scrubbing the tiled floor, polishing the furniture and mirrors, checking supplies, changing the towels. All that remains finally is the making of the bed. But how can she do that, she worries, standing there in the afternoon sunlight with stacks of crisp clean sheets in her arms like empty ledgers, her virtuous resolve sapped by a gathering sense of dread as penetrating and aseptic as ammonia, if the master won't get out of it?

She enters, encumbered with her paraphernalia, which she deposits by the wall near the door, crosses the room (circumspectly, precipitately, etc.), and flings open the garden doors,

smashing the glass, as though once and
for all. "Teach me, my God and King,"
she remarks ruefully (such a sweet breath
of amicable violence all about!), "in all
things thee to–oh! I beg your pardon,
sir!" "A . . . a dream," he stammers,
squinting in the glare. He is bound tightly
in the damp sheets, can barely move.
"Something about blood and a . . . a . . .
I'm so old, and still each day–" "Sir . . . ?"
He clears his throat. "Would you look under the bed, please, and tell me what you
see?" "I–I'm sorry, sir," she replies, kneel-
ing down to look, a curious strained expression on her face. With a scream, she
disappears. He awakes, his heart pounding. The maid is staring down at his erection as though frightened of his righteous
ardor: "Oh, I beg your pardon, sir!" "It's
nothing . . . a dream," he explains, rising
like the pink clouds of dawn. "Something
about . . ." But he can no longer remember, his mind is a blank sheet. Anyway, she

is no longer listening. He can hear her moving busily about the room, dusting furniture, sweeping the floor, changing the towels, taking a shower. He's standing there abandoned to the afternoon sunlight in his slippers and pajama bottoms, which seem to have imbibed an unhealthy kind of dampness, when a bird comes in and perches on his erection, what's left of it. "Ah–!" "Oh, I beg your pardon, sir!" "It's–it's nothing," he replies hoarsely, blinking up at her, gripped still by claws as fine as waxed threads. "A dream . . ." But she has left him, gone off singing to her God and King. He tries to pull the blanket back over his head (the bird, its beak opening and closing involuntarily like spanked thighs, was brown as a chestnut, he recalls, and still smoldering, but she returns and snatches it away, the sheets too. Sometimes she can be too efficient. Maybe he has been pushing her too hard, expecting too much too soon. He sits up, feeling rudely exposed (his erection dips back into his pajamas like a frog diving for cover—indeed, it has a greenish cast to it in the half-light of the curtained room: what? isn't she here yet?), and lowers his feet over the side, shuffling dutifully for his slippers. But he can't find them. He can't even find the floor! He jerks back, his skin wrinkling in involuntary panic, but feels the bottom sheet slide out from under him— "What? *WHAT—?!*" "Oh, I beg your pardon, sir!" "Ah ... it's nothing," he gasps, struggling to awaken, his heart pounding still (it should be easier than this!), as, screaming, she tucks up her skirt. "A dream ..."

She enters, as though once and for all, circumspectly deposits her vital paraphernalia beside the door, then crosses the room to fling open (humbly yet authoritatively) the curtains and the garden doors: there is such a song of birds all about! Excited by that, and by the sweet breath of late afternoon, her own eagerness to serve, and faith in the perfectibility of her tasks, she turns with a glad heart and tosses back the bedcovers: "Oh! I beg your pardon, sir!" "A . . . a dream," he mutters gruffly, his erection slipping back inside his pajamas like an abandoned moral. "Something about glory and a pizzle—or puzzle—and a fundamental position in the civil service . . ." But she is no longer listening, busy now at her common round, dusting furniture and sweeping the floor: so much to do! When (not very willingly, she observes) he leaves the bed at last, she strips the sheets and blankets off, shaking the dead bees into the garden, fluffs and airs the pillows, turns the mattress. She hears the master relieving himself noisily in the bathroom: yes,

there's water in the bucket, soap too, a
sponge, she's remembered everything! Today then, perhaps at last . . ! Quickly she
polishes the mirror, mops the floor, snaps
open the fresh sheets and makes the bed.
Before she has the spread down, however,
he comes out of the bathroom, staggers
across the room muttering something
about "a bloody new birth," and crawls
back into it. "But, sir–!" "What, what?"
he yawns, and rolls over on his side, pulling the blanket over his head. She
snatches it away. He sits up, blinking, a
curious strained expression on his face.
"I–I'm sorry, sir," she says, and, pushing
her drawers down to her knees, tucking
her skirt up and bending over, she pre-
sents to him that broad part preferred by
him and Mother Nature for the invention
of souls. He retrieves the blanket and disappears under it, all but his feet, which
stick out at the bottom, still slippered. She
stuffs her drawers hastily behind her apron

bib, knocks over the mop bucket, smears
the mirror, throws the fresh towels in the
toilet, and jerks the blanket away again.
"I—I'm sorry, sir," she insists, bending
over and lifting her skirt: "I'm sure I had
them on when I came in . . ." What? Is he
snoring? She peers at him past what is
now her highest part, that part invaded
suddenly by a dread as chilling as his chastisements are, when true to his manuals,
enflaming, and realizes with a faint shudder (she cannot hold back the little explosions of wind) that change and condition
are coeval and everlasting: a truth as hol-
low as the absence of birdsong (but they
are singing!) . . .

So she stands there in
the open doorway, the glass doors having
long since been flung open (when was

that? she cannot remember), her thighs taut and pressed closely together, her face buried in his cast-off pajamas. She can feel against her cheeks, her lips, the soft consoling warmth of them, so recently relinquished, can smell in them the terror—no, the painful sadness, the divine drudgery (sweet, like crushed flowers, dead birds)— of his dreams, Mother Nature having provided, she knows all too well, the proper place for what God has ordained. But there is another odor in them too, musty, faintly sour, like that of truth or freedom, the fear of which governs every animal, thereby preventing natural confusion and disorder. Or so he has taught her. Now, her face buried in this pungent warmth and her heart sinking, the comforting whirr and smack of his rod no more than a distant echo, disappearing now into the desolate throb of late-afternoon birdsong, she wonders about the manuals, his service to them and hers to him, or to that beyond him which he has not quite named. Whence such an appetite?—she shudders, groans, chewing helplessly on the pajamas—so little relief?

Distantly blows are falling, something about freedom and government, but he is strolling in the garden with a teacher he once had, discussing the condition of humanity, which keeps getting mixed up somehow with homonymity, such that each time his teacher issues a new lament it comes out like slapped laughter. He is about to remark on the generous swish and snap of a morning glory that has sprung up in their path as though inspired ("Paradox, too, has its techniques," his teacher is saying, "and so on . . ."), when it turns out to be a woman he once knew on the civil surface. "What?

WHAT−?!" But she only wants him to change his position, or perhaps his condition ("You see!" remarks his teacher sagely, unbuckling his belt, "it's like a kind of callipygomancy, speaking loosely−am I being unfair?"), he's not sure, but anyway it doesn't matter, for what she really wants is to get him out of the sheets he's wrapped in, turn him over (he seems to have imbibed an unhealthy kind of dampness), and give him a lecture (she says "elixir") on method and fairies, two dew-bejeweled habits you can roast chestnuts over. What more, really, does he want of her? (Perhaps his teacher asks him this, buzzing in and out of his ear like the sweet breath of solemnity: whirr-*SMACK!*) His arm is rising and falling through great elastic spaces as though striving for something fundamental like a forgotten dream or lost drawers. "I−I'm sorry, sir!" Is she testing him, perched there on his stout engine of duty like a

cooked bird with the lingering bucket of
night in her beak (see how it opens,
closes, opens), or is it only a dimpled fever
of the mind? He doesn't know, is almost
afraid to ask. "Something about a higher
end," he explains hoarsely, taking rueful
refuge, "or hired end perhaps, and boiled
flowers, hard parts—and another thing,
what's left of it . . ." She screams. The
garden groans, quivers, starts, its groves
radiant and throbbing. His teacher, no
longer threatening, has withdrawn discreetly to a far corner with diagonal
creases, where he is turning what lilacs
remain into roses with his rumpled bull's
pizzle: it's almost an act of magic! Still his
arm rises and falls, rises and falls, that
broad part of Mother Nature destined for
such inventions dancing and bobbing soft
and easy under the indulgent sun: "It's a
beautiful day!" "What? *WHAT—?!* An
answering back to a reproof?" he inquires
gratefully, taunting her with that civility

and kindness due to an inferior, as—hiss-
WHAP!—flicking lint off one shoulder
and smoothing the ends of his moustache
with involuntary vertical and horizontal
motions, he floats helplessly backwards
("Thank you, sir!"), twitching amicably
yet authoritatively like a damp towel,
down a bottomless hole, relieving himself
noisily: *"Perhaps today then . . . at last!"*